Published by Kingly Books, Glasgow.
www.kinglybooks.com

John Bagnall: mail@bagpen.fsnet.co.uk

'Termite Fraternity' appeared in 'Atlantic Garage' (1987).
'S.O.S. Esther' appeared in 'Escape' no.13 (1987).
'English Oral' appeared in 'Gag' no.7 (1989).
'Get My Own Groceries' appeared in 'Off The Road' (1996).
'A Nation Of Shopkeepers' was published as a booklet (2000).
All other artwork and stories appear here for the first time,
©2003 John Bagnall.

Foreword ©2003 Seth.

ISBN: 0 9531 6392 X

All rights reserved. No part of this book (except for small portions for review purposes) may be reproduced, stored in a retrieval system or transmitted in any form or by any means, without the prior permission in writing of John Bagnall. Nor be otherwise circulated in any form of binding or cover other than that in which it is published and without a similar condition, including this condition, being imposed on the subsequent purchaser.

Printed by Clydeside Press, Glasgow.

Discovering John Bagnall's work is like coming across a marvellous second-hand shop on a rarely frequented street. You wander in, start digging about, and are soon rewarded with remarkable finds. You can't help lament that you hadn't found this place earlier. Much like that second-hand shop, John's work is a wonderful hodge-podge of cultural flotsam and jetsam (past and present) pulled together in a genuinely unique way.

I first came across John's work in the late 80's in Escape magazine and was immediately won over by its obvious charm and eccentricity. Alongside his contemporaries Dakin, Reynolds, Elliot, etc., creating a subtle yet vibrant form of British comics, a sensibility rooted in the mundane but full of surrealism, whimsy and mystery. It seems a shame that so little of this work has made its way over the ocean in the preceding decade. That's why this new collection of his work is such a welcomed gift.

Seth.
North Guelph,
Canada.
May 2003.

TABLE OF CONTENTS

The Chemist and the Capuchin
Cecil lived in the English suburbs, but why couldn't he resist the call of a strange monk in the Italian mountains?

Get My Own Groceries
David Bowie once had to flee the limelight. Here are the facts of his stay in West Berlin.

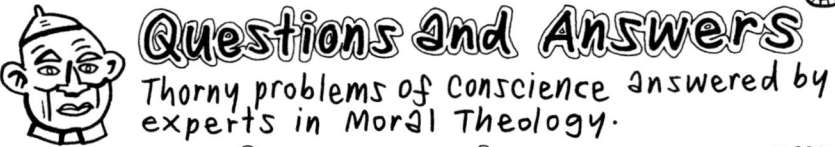

Questions and Answers
Thorny problems of conscience answered by experts in Moral Theology.

Termite Fraternity
Across the Atlantic something stirs underneath Atticus College---

Our Lady of the Tower Block
Landing a teaching job at Our Lady of Fatima turned out to be Miss Buchanan's biggest mistake.

Nation of Shopkeepers
Will that be an ice-cream sandwich or a short Back'n'Sides?

S.O.S. Esther
Vintage account of of a young girl's attempt to break the ties of an unhappy childhood.

The town I live in / Colour Slide
Two records from the 1960's - partly illustrated.

Northern Holiday
Cousin Raymond undergoes the Pit Village experience and comes out smiling.

English Oral
Early slice of autobiography. Where is Tina Lyons now?

Disappearing Phrases
Improve your word power with these lovingly preserved sayings.

I felt pain--intense pain--but not for long. Stillness followed--the stillness of the country night.

I could see through what seemed like mountains, but were in fact shattered glass chips, lit by the moon--

Then the queerest experience--floating above the scene, I could observe all of the wreckage.

I watched two cars slow down--then pass.

Finally, and mercifully, a farmers wagon stopped--

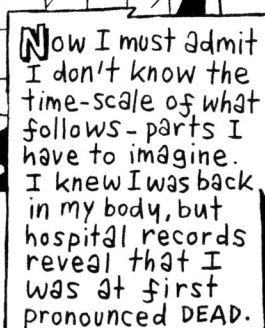

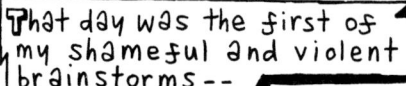

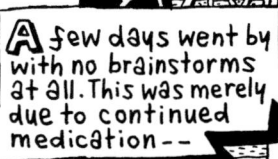

MONDAY — HERE I AM IN EUROPE -- WEST BERLIN TO BE EXACT -- CUT OFF FROM MY OLD LIFE AND RARING TO GO. BUT WHERE AM I GOING TO LIVE? DECIDED TO PHONE MY NEW CHUM ENO IN LONDON.

MY NEW HOME IS IN NEUKÖLN — A RUN DOWN PART OF THE CITY WHERE TURKISH IMMIGRANTS LIVE -- FOUND A GAFF ABOVE AN AUTO SHOP WHICH SEEMS CHEAP -- PAINTED IT IN MY FAVOURITE COLOUR -- BLUE.

BERLIN HAS BARS FULL OF THE DEPRESSED & DISILLUSIONED -- I GET DRUNK ON MY OWN AND SOAK UP THE ATMOSPHERE -- PROBLEM IS I'M NOT AS ANONYMOUS AS I'D LIKE -- TIME TO STAY IN?

MUSIC CAN WAIT BUT I'M PAINTING -- SELF PORTRAITS IN THE STYLE OF EGON SHIELE -- SOME DAYS I JUST LIE AND STARE AT THE WALL. BLIMEY, I THINK I'M BECOMING A TRUE ISOLATED BERLINER --

WE MADE IT THROUGH THE IRON CURTAIN AND HAD A GREAT DAY. EAST BERLIN HAS A REPRESSED FEELING -- SOMETHING BOILING UNDER --
Bleak--
Hey Honey--wanta date with a capitalist? Hyuh, Hyuh!
Coff
These window displays are so minimalist--
BROT
Let's find a bar!
SATURDAY - I WOKE AND IGGY HAD LEFT -- OFF ON ANOTHER ADVENTURE. A PARCEL FROM ENO --- HIS GIFT MAKES SOME INTRIGUING NOISES --
Iggy?
Corblimey--its an ARP synthesiser!
Herr Bowie-- you pay carriage charge--
BOWIE
121 STRASS
WEEEEBRR
ARP
Yep--I can write some tunes with this!
John Bagnall © 96.

Q. Did I read once in your Magazine that a person can write to the Pope? If so, what address would I write to, and how should I address the Pope?
Q. Do our dead friends know how lonely we are on earth after they die and leave us alone? Do they know when another member of the family dies?
Q. Are our Guardian Angels outside the heavenly paradise, but with the beatific vision (As Our Lord had from the moment of birth) or do they guard us from their thrones in Heaven. Can they be in two places at once.
Q. I thought that God forgives everybody their sins, but if so, why is there a Purgatory and Hell?
Q. My daughter has been a nun for ten years, and was finally professed for three years. About two years ago she got unsettled and very recently decided to come home. Her father and myself are very upset.
Q. For some time past I say my Prayers in bed or sitting on a chair. I would like to know if my prayers are heard with the same reverence as if I had said them on my knees.
Q. I went to Confession but could not hear the Penance the priest gave me. Should I go to Confession again and tell my sins again?
Q. Where could I get a blue scapular of the Immaculate Conception?
Q. A while ago my father died after a long illness. That same night my friend told me he had heard loud knocking on his window. I wonder would the knocking have any relation to my father's death?

A. There is nothing to stop one writing directly to the Pope. His address is Vatican City, The Vatican. You could begin you letter, 'Holy Father'.
A. Our dead friends know what God allows them to know. Having lived on earth they are presumably aware of the after death loneliness of those who are left.
A. Angels have no bodies. Therefore they are not in place. Thus an Angel could be in several places at the one time. Our Guardian Angels are in heaven in that they have the Beatific Vision — this is what is meant by Heaven.
A. God forgives everybody their sins, but of course they must be sorry for the sins. If they commit mortal sins but do not repent for having them, they go to Hell.
A. The fact that her health and her nerves were unable to stand the strain any longer is no reflection upon her or upon you. She did what God wanted to be done for as long as He wished her to do it.
A. Not at all. Pray on your knees. You may find this difficult at the beginning, but in your case it is essential.
A. Not at all. Say the usual Penance the priest gives and that will suffice.
A. We suggest you ask the Clerk of the Church where you usually go to Mass. Usually the Clerk knows exactly where Religious Goods are available.
A. I am very sorry to hear of your predicament. Please pray hard for the courage and faith you need.

TeRmiTe Fraternity

Something went wrong one semester at Atticus State College--

Fall came and the freshmen were settling in as normal...

Time-honored entry rituals to Fraternity houses took place:

13hr marathons of Ravel's "Bolero." "Crank it up!"

Hunting for the non-existent college-pin--

Having your underwear hung on the college weather-vane "Haw Haw!"

But in Phi-Beta-Kappa house the rules were different--

"So you want to be Phi-Beta-Kappa members? As you'll know for 150 years this has been the college elite!"

"--and to become a member the rituals are a little more -- rigorous! Anyone know much about termites?"

Hallo Pop? hey in a week from now I may be a real member of Phi Beta Kappa -- Yep! your old house!
MATH
Pledging obedience to the fraternity head the eager students were ordered to imitate termite behaviour--
termitus
Harrison and Cheever! Tunnel C!
They dug tunnels under the campus.
Some dropped out--
Ugh! Is the frat-head a zoology student or a nut?
While most continued in their quest for social status!
Only 2 days to go!
The frat-head's secret plan could then have come true:
To undermine the college's foundations and cause its collapse!
But who'd have predicted the visiting building inspectors?
Tut Tut.
And who'd have predicted the change from Big Man on campus to hated social-outcast?
Communist!
Vandal!
Crazy Son of a Bitch
END.

A FAIRFIELD PARADE episode

TERESA! Give me those bloody clacker things NOW.

KLAK

These are CONFISCATED! They've been giving me a HEADACHE all day---

But Miss, They're MINE!

HIGH SPIRITED young souls are'nt they Miss Buchanan?

Oh-- I didn't see you there, Sister Scholastica!

It's a difficult age for them-- Puberty causes such CONFUSION.

And some of their PARENTS-- I swear HALF OF THEM don't go to MASS anymore!

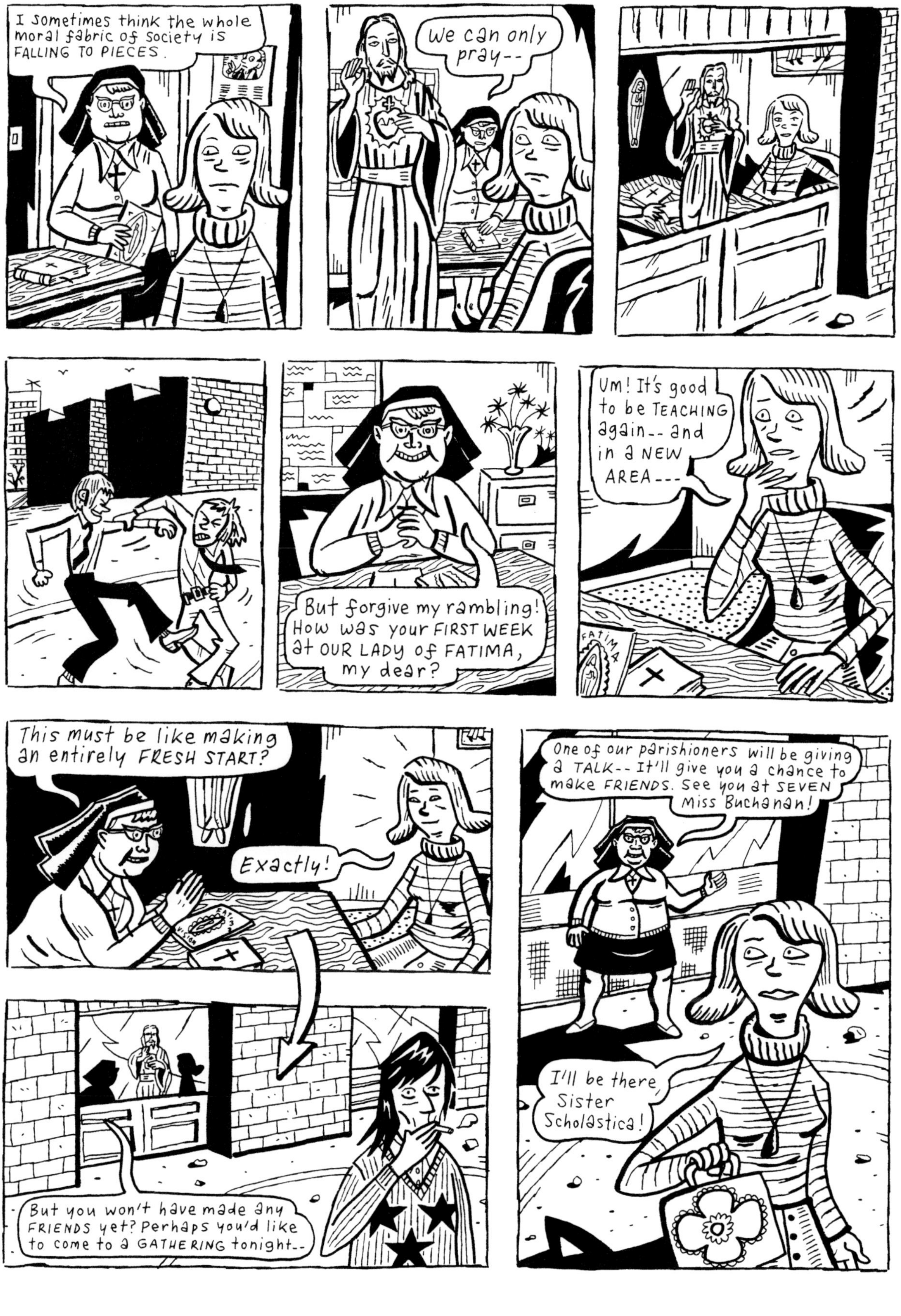

OUR LADY OF THE TOWER BLOCK

CONVENT OF OUR LADY OF FATIMA
TALK 7PM
LITTER
≡gasp≡ Sorry I'm a bit late--My name's Miss Buchanan!
That's alright. I'm Sister Catherine--I think that Brendan Cass has just started--
MARIA
CONCEIVED WITHOUT SIN
Now sisters, I don't need to tell you why we should be devoted to Our Blessed Lady the VIRGIN MARY--
But let us remember JESUS only came into our world through the CONSENT and CO-OPERATION of this very SPECIAL LADY--
--without His MOTHER MARY there would be no CHRIST of CALVARY
--just as without MOTHERS today there would be no PRIESTS to stand "in persona Christi" in our HOLY MASS!
Women's role as MOTHERS or CARERS is also recognised in the title "Our Holy MOTHER the Church."
≡Hic≡
But most of all dear sisters
we can be sure that Mary, our HEAVENLY Mother watches over us and hears our daily honour and praise!
≡Hic≡

Immaculate Mary --our hearts are on fire
--that title so wondrous fills all our desires.
Ah--lovely! What a rousing finish to another inspiring evening with our friend Brendan Cass--
We are blessed to have such a gifted and charismatic young man in this parish.
Come along, you MUST meet our newest teacher!
!
Hi!
Brendan, this is MISS BUCHANAN.
Pleased to ≡hic≡ meet you.
I couldn't help NOTICING you as you sat there. What a HEALTHY GLOW you have, Miss Buchanan.
Can I give you a lift HOME perhaps?
Er no--I can walk it.
You MUST ACCEPT, Miss Buchanan!
The streets of Fairfield Parade aren't as SAFE as they used to be--
Yes, Our Lady of Fatima is a fine school-I went there myself.
HONDA
This is my tower block Mr. Cass
OK
Less of the MISTER next time--I hope I'll be seeing a LOT MORE of you. God Bless!
≡hic≡ Thanks.

≥click≤ the sound of Barry Blue there. Morning, Guys and Gals -- I-i-it's Saturday!!
Remember folks, there's Go-Karting at Fairfield Stadium today and---
tonight Picketty Witch are appearing at Chaplin's Night Club.
Hello, could I book a hair appointment for eleven?
--Yeh. What's the name chuck?
Miss Buchanan.
So how about a curly perm? They're really coming in this year--
CURLY BIRDS
No thanks, I just want a trim.
So chuck, you're one of the teachers at Our Lady of Fatima? My Katie'n' Kevin go there--
Do they?
Some of the sisters are lovely, but--
Crikey!
CURLY
Are you ALRIGHT, chuck?
Er, yes! What were you saying?
--that SISTER SCHOLASTICA can be a bit of a cow.

See you again chuck.
Yes, Bye.
Miss Buchanan?
Bloody Hell.
That's alright--I'm sure we hear worse from some of our pupils don't we?
Sorry I gave you a SHOCK.
Um--I'm a little JUMPY. Mustn't have SLEPT well last night--or something.
--Are you OK?
Oh. Yes! Excuse my language, Sister catherine.
Did last night with the SISTERS have that effect on you?
WHAT? Oh no, of course not---Well, it is all NEW to me-you see I've never taught in a CONVENT SCHOOL before.
Oh.
In that case BRENDAN CASS must also be a NEW EXPERIENCE to you. He's so full of the HOLY SPIRIT isn't he?
Sister Scholastica thinks the WORLD of him.
I'm SURE sister will invite you to FUTURE GATHERINGS, Miss Buchanan--

--and besides I think BRENDAN CASS has taken QUITE A SHINE to you!
MILLIG
OFF LICENCE
Hello Luv, I suppose it's a bottle of QUEEN OF SHEBA?
No.
I suppose it's TWO bloody bottles of QUEEN OF SHEBA.
y'know you wanna GO EASY on this stuff, girl.
Perhaps I'll go easy on it when you go easy on PIES AND CHIPS!
'Ey calm down girl. At least I'm not a ruddy--ALKY!
!

Panel 1: (BAZ, FIRE signs on wall)

Panel 2: (woman climbing stairs, shadow on wall)

Panel 3: "Ah, God Bless you."

Panel 4: "Eeek!"

Panel 5: "Forgive me, I seem to have given you a fright--"

Panel 6: "Were these bottles YOURS?" "Yes."

Panel 7: "Here, let me help. I was trying to find YOUR FLAT, and invite you to another TALK I'm giving at the SISTERS tomorrow night--"

Panel 8: "This one's about the amazing apparitions of our BLESSED MOTHER MARY at Fatima."

Panel 9: "Can I come INSIDE and tell you some MORE?"

Panel 10: "What! Er no-- I've got lessons to prepare."

Panel 11: "Alright Miss Buchanan. See you tomorrow-- and remember-- A prayer to our Lady is an aid to all kinds of --PROBLEMS."

Remember, before you go home tonight--
--that CLACKERS are now totally BANNED in this school, since Sister Concepta's accident.
Aw.
Boo.
OK, class DISMISSED-- and be QUIET about it!
Miss?
Yes?
I just wanted to say your HAIR looks SMASHING.
I'm sorry--?
I'm Katie Kennedy. My Mam runs Curly Birds.
The hairdressers? Oh yes-- I was there on Saturday.
That's right, Miss. And here's my older brother Kevin--
Hello Kevin.
Hiya Miss.
Anyhow, our Mam just wanted to say--
--that you're welcome to call in for a cup of TEA anytime.
Thanks! I will.
Yeh, you don't have to get your hair done or anything!
Miss Buchanan.
Sister Catherine?
Sister Scholastica wants to see you in her office, Miss Buchanan.
I think it's quite serious.

Panel 1: (Miss Buchanan stands in a hallway, a schoolgirl visible behind her.)

Panel 2:
Sister: Come inside and sit down.
Sister: I expect you have a GOOD IDEA of why I've called you to my office Miss Buchanan.

Panel 3:
Buchanan: Not really, Sister.
Sister: If you must be coy about it I will tell you--
Sister: You did NOT attend last night's GATHERING.

Panel 4:
Buchanan: I didn't realise it was compulsory.

Panel 5:
Sister: I thought I had already explained the ETHOS of this school to you

Panel 6:
Sister: Both the convent and the school are a COMMUNITY! All newcomers--
Sister: --especially those who are UNMARRIED, are WELCOMED into the COMMUNITY.

Panel 7:
Sister: Yet you are already REJECTING our offers of friendship--or perhaps you had OTHER things to do--
Sister: Perhaps you were drinking BOTTLES OF SHERRY!?

Panel 8:
Buchanan: I'll tell you why I didn't come, Sister Scholastica. Because your precious BRENDAN CASS is stalking me!
Sister: Rubbish!

Panel 9:
Buchanan: It's true--he's a CREEP and a PERVERT!
Sister: Shut up!
Sister: Shut up! You're a --DIRTY WOMAN!

Panel 10:
Sister: I have no option but to SUSPEND you--- Get out!
Buchanan: OK.

Go on chuck-- Have another CUSTARD CREAM.
OK, I will.
COOP CUSTARD
So now I KNOW why you were a BAG OF NERVES the first time you came here.
And now things are even worse!
crunch
CO-OP CUSTARD
Look darlin', I don't think Sister Scholastica has ANY grounds to give you the BOOT.
She'll calm down-- you've just slagged off her GOLDEN BOY that's all.
Maybe.
But there's-- the SHERRY DRINKING.
Brendan Cass must have told HER about that.
If them NUNS were as HOLY as they look they'd try to HELP you, not put you down.
I do TRY to cut down-- but it's hard with all this pressure
Look Chuck, do you FEEL BETTER for getting this OFF YOUR CHEST?
I do!
Hello?
Oh, frig. Here's a CUSTOMER.
Call in TOMORROW, eh? And tell me if there's any NEWS--
I will, Elvina.

Oh, and TRY NOT TO WORRY too much, eh?
Things WILL get better.
"y'Know you wanna GO EASY on this stuff, girl--"
"Shut up! You're a DIRTY WOMAN!"
"Can I come inside and tell you some more?"
BAM! Oh, hi Miss-- are you coming back to SCHOOL?
Yes, I think so, Barry.
That's GOOD Miss!
It's a beautiful warm September afternoon here in Fairfield--
Why not make a cuppa and put up your feet during this one--
zzzzz
Ah, God Bless you Miss Buchanan.
© John BAGnall 2003

A NATION OF SHOPKEEPERS

JOHN BAGNALL

SUPER MARKET

RECORD SHOP
STYLOPHONE
9d
VALIANT
TOP 20
EMITEX
WOW! BRASS
SOUNDS LIKE STRING
MEXICO
STEREO
CLASSIC MOODS

BARBERS
STYPTIC PENCIL
LIST
DUREX
WEBBS
SERVICE
RAC
PARTS
VITALIS
SNOOPFIX

ICE CREAM PARLOUR
OFTEN LICKED - NEVER BEATEN
FRIGICHEST

TAILORS
NCP

SHOE SHOP

BOUTIQUE

TOY SHOP
NASA
MOON SHOT
DR WHO
DINKY
CHINESE CHECKERS
WE SELL FUZZY FELT
Tri-ang
PUSH AND GO!
Sindy

BUTCHERS
BRITISH BEEF
BRITISH IS BEST

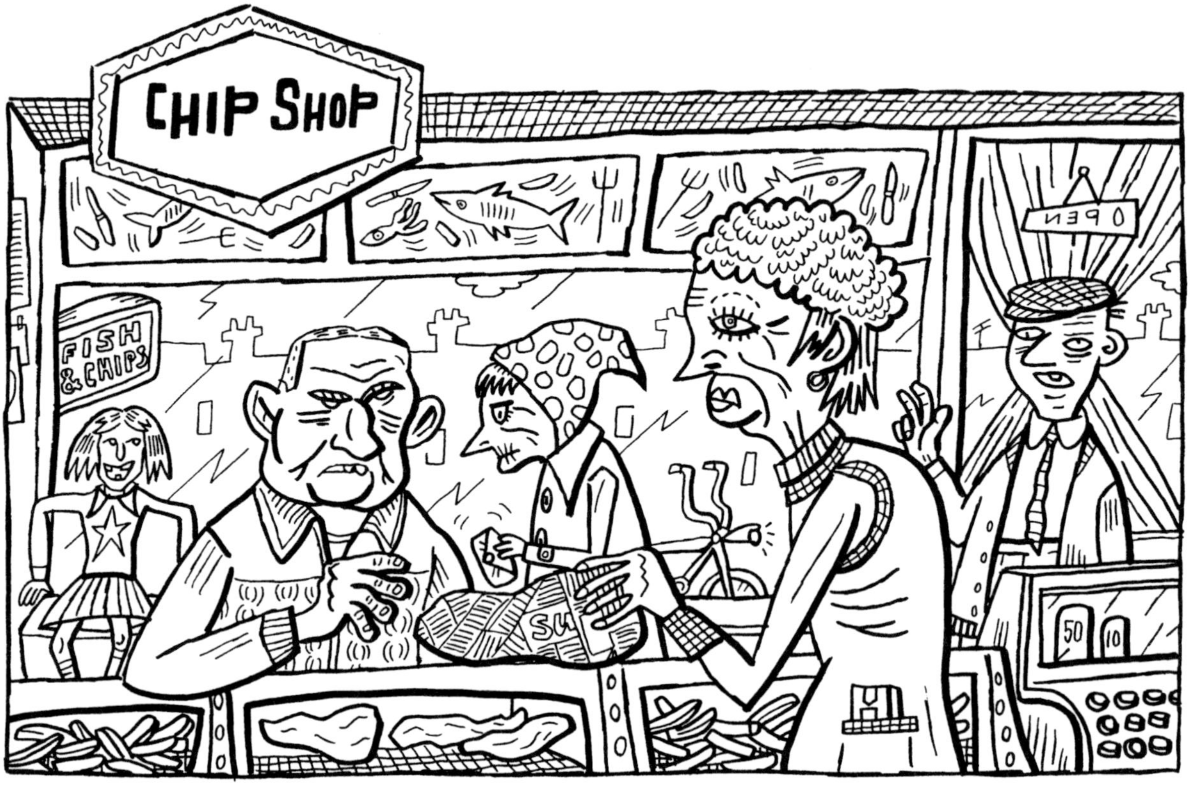
CHIP SHOP
FISH & CHIPS

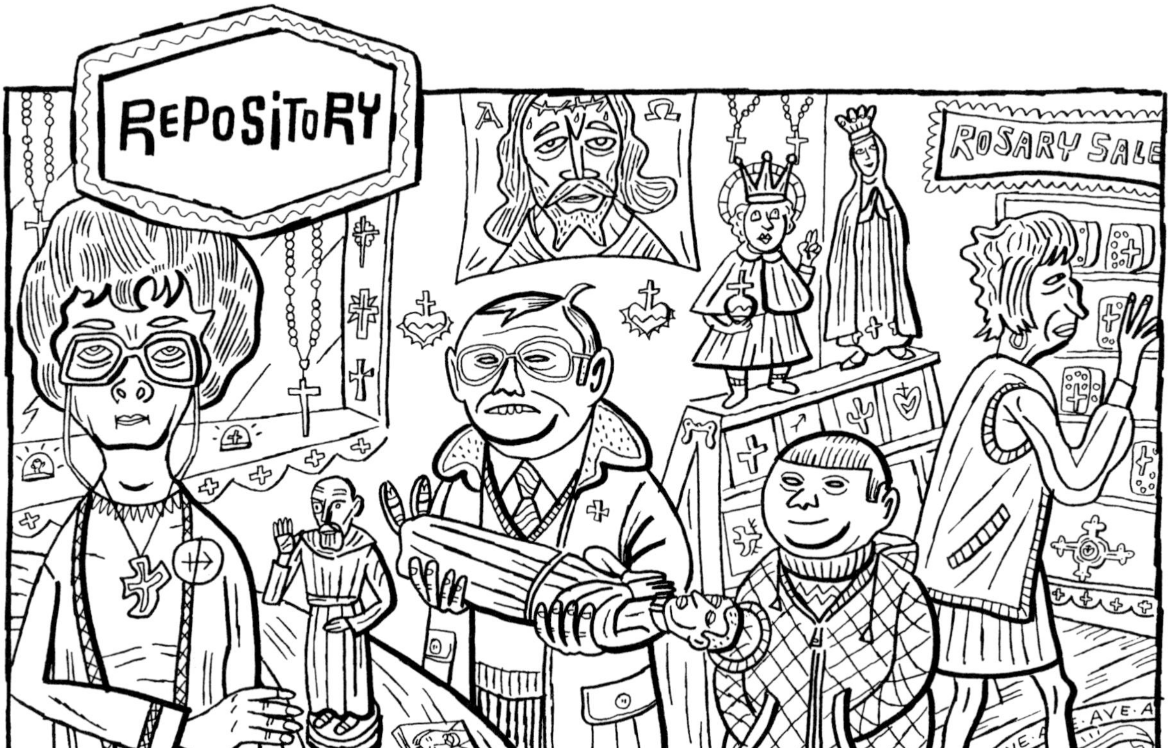
REPOSITORY
ROSARY SALE

S.O.S. ESTHER
RRINNG RRIINNG
RRIING RRIINNG
Grrowl!
≡yawn≡ quiet now Buster – it's 2 a.m.--
RRING!!
Woof!
--Hello?
--MOTHER!!
Don't sound so alarmed Esther, Yes it's your MOTHER, who you haven't contacted in 3 weeks!
Er.. I've been busy, my job--
Um--how are you?
Give me a break
If you were CONCERNED dear you'd know I'm sick--dangerously sick!

Of course I'm concerned -- You're really sick?
Don't abandon me again Esther coff coff
I'll get in my car straight away!
12
13
vrrooomm
was it really 18 years ago?
Esther meet your new mother!

Ray, was your first wife a midget?
Ssh Hon-- Esther's still upset about her real mother's death. She's a sensitive kid!
Wear your hair up Esther - You've got to make the best of what you've got--'cos girl you ain't got much!
HONK!
ACME
Holy Joe! I nearly crashed while reminiscing
I'm so tired and--it's so far to Mother's
SEATOWN
ACCOMODATION AHEAD 300 YARDS
I'll have to rest for a few hours yawn This place should be OK!
Hitchcock Chalets
VACANCIES

RECEPTION
Hello! Er--you do accept pets dont you?
How long will you be staying?
Just until the morning-- I'm travelling to Seatown --my Mother's sick.
Sick?--You may use my phone if you wish.
Hello? I'm on my way.
coff where are you now?
I'm at a motel called Hitchcock Chalets--I can't drive all night!
coff you always were lazy coff I'm getting weaker.
I'll drive again in a few hours
Chop chop Esther, you have to earn your keep somehow!
--Mother I've finished
About time! Now sit in the yard I have a visitor--
--but where's Daddy?
At work--now BUZZ OFF!

"Mother," I HATE YOU!
OH--IS it morning again?
Cripes, It's SEVEN!
So long! I must be on my way!
Of course Ma'am
Mother, I have an opportunity in Dynamo plains as a stenographer--
What? That's nearly a 100 miles away!
You're just trying to shirk your duties especially now your father's gone!
---Besides ...I'm not a well woman anymore--
You're Lying.
You're as fit as I am!
SLAP!
That's IT. I'm going NOW! =sob=

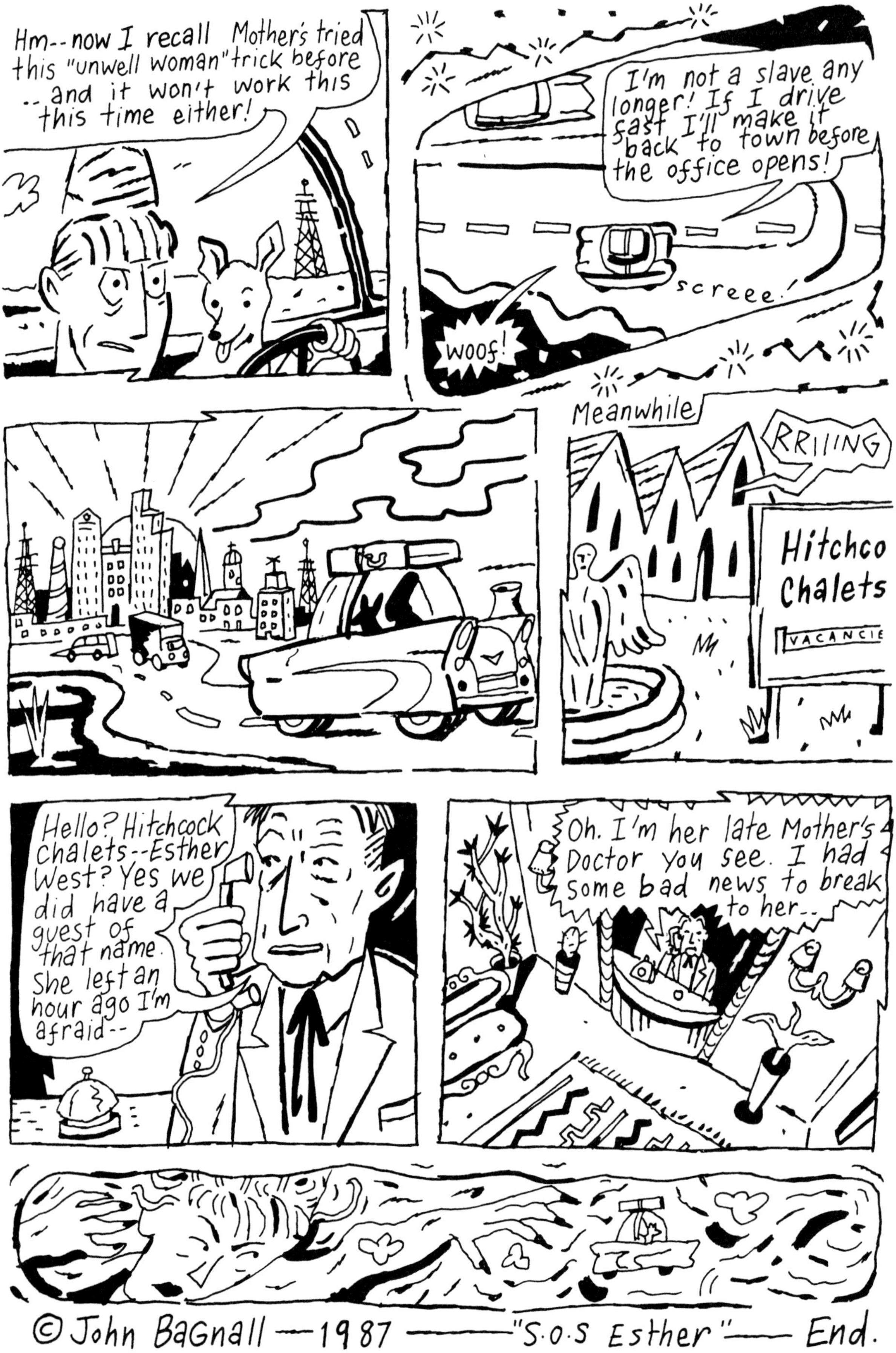

© John BaGnall —— 1987 —————— "S.O.S Esther" —— End.

'The Town I Live In' Jackie Lee (Columbia Records)

'Colour Slide' The Honeycombs (RGM Productions)

Hose down the Pit-Head Baths! Here comes Cousin Raymond on his
NORTHERN HOLIDAY
RAY
Auntie Olive and Uncle Wilf, 125 Co-operative Terrace.
CAPSTAN NAVY CUT CIGARETTES
What's this grub, Auntie Olive?
Best Ham Shank and Pease Pudding
Shh. Great Auntie is polishing her Coronation spoon.
BRASSO
Cor! Uncle Wilf's Pigeons--

No two pigeons are the same, young Raymond. Take Woodbine Tessie here.
Coo!
Monday is always washing Day-- Come and help me peg out Uncle Wilf's Linings *
* Underwear.
--And here's me prize Leeks, nearly ready for showing
Gigantic!
Sundays, Great Auntie & Me go to Chapel--
WESLEYAN CHAPEL
Your Uncle Wilf goes to the Club.
Belch.
--then it's time for more pease Pudding!
A TIME MACHINE TRAVELOGUE

ENGLISH ORAL

Tina Lyons • Mr. Murray • Simon Ness • Me

© John Bagnall

Panel 1: My fourth year at school—
"Gak"

Panel 2: and we had a new English teacher—
"Like Hi, I'm Mr. Murray. If you treat me OK I'll do likewise.— No need to call me SIR."
Denim suit

Panel 3: He outlined his approach to us—
"The School I went to was just like an EXAM FACTORY— I want you to be TRULY CREATIVE and er— SPEAK, Right?"

Panel 4: He was desperate to be on the same level as "the Kids."
"Hi John— wot's your album? Hey, have you heard The Grateful Dead?"
"Like TO-O-TALLY TASTY!"

Panel 5: Mr. Murray GRATED on most of us.
"He's a drippy hippie!"
"A furry GONK"

Panel 6: Next week he announced we all had to do a speech: an English Oral.
"Sir, can we talk about STARSKY & HUTCH?"
"Yeh— ANYTHING. I wanta see where YOU'RE COMING FROM!"

Hanging around afterwards, some of us discussed what subject we were going to speak on ---
Think I'll do NUDIE BOOKS.
nearest she'd been to a horse was watching "Follyfoot" on TV.
ooh NO. HORSE RIDING is much more suitable!
I'M NOT DOING ONE.
My choice was easy. I had become obsessed with vampires (there'd been Hammer re-runs on TV.)
My favourite vampire film was "Dracula A.D. 1972": it starred Christopher Lee and a mob of teenagers in flares
Ooh--Dracula you're a real TASTY GEEZER!
DESIST, wench!
and the biggest compliment my parents could pay me was:
Why don't you get some fresh air?
You look like Death warmed up----
No, I don't like DAYLIGHT, but here is some money. Please buy me "Tomb of Dracula" while you're out--
The first day of the orals came, and I was one of the earliest.
OK John, Go ahead.
Er--do vampires really exist?
petrified
Afterwards:
That was OK John, but you didn't put enuff of YOURSELF into it--
You see, I want you to learn SELF-EXPRESSION!
You'll learn something one of these DARK NIGHTS

Let down by Murray's reaction. I was interested to see what would follow--
Next, Simon Ness.
Speaking on--?
GOLF.
Simon Ness was hooked on Golf because
FORE!
his Dad ran a sweet shop on Bowring park Golf course.
Ahem
ENGLISH ORALS
LFC
The rules of Golf are
Through nerves, Simon was swinging his legs--
quite simple really
snork
giggle
Half of us were hypnotised, the others creased up in laughter.
swish
OK OK, COOL IT everybody--Give Simon a break!
HAW
HAW
Hee HA
Hee
Right, we'll have another, if you stop hassling me--
Tina Lyons?
Tina Lyons was a quiet, sullen girl. No-one really knew her well.
sac
BIOLOGY
She didn't have any close friends.
The start of her oral: "My Holiday" was pretty dull--
Last Summer, My Dad, Sister and I went to Corn-wall.
My Dad did the driving.
CORNWALL
yawn

the weather was quite hot and I felt sleepy. We carried on driving west--
Exciting eh?
We found ourselves stopped in a traffic-jam. "Wonder what the hold-up is," asked my Dad. "I'll go and have a look," I said. I got out of the car and walked on about 100 yards. I could see there'd been a serious CRASH between two cars--
CORNWALL
I walked closer-- Four passengers were DEAD in the wreckage.
ULP
They were smothered in BLOOD ----
One had a SMASHED SKULL
think I'm going to faint
the brain was showing..
Tina's monotone oral droned on, despite Karen Wickstead FAINTING and Stephen Dix being SICK.
OK Tina.. I think you'd better STOP!
the brain looked grey and soft, with--
dark red creases--
STOP Stop!
CORNWALL
For the first time I felt sorry for Mr. Murray--
Sir, Derek has FAINTED too
STOP
There was no more "self-expression" for quite a while.
Right everybody, Act One Scene Two.
SHAKESPEARE
THE WORKS
A true story from BAGGY STUDIOS

DISAPPEARING PHRASES

As heard by John Bagnall

He'd talk a glass eye asleep.

She'd eat one more potato than a pig.

It's a Top Coat warmer today, Mrs Snoopdale.
ESOLDO
PARK
ICES
SOUND FOOD VALUE
STOP ME & BUY ONE
TUBS 3D BRICKS 6D

Now you're really gettin' on my wick.
Oh, shut your cakehole!
PEPSI

Shoes
She's put the beef on--
HALF PRICE SALE
and he couldn't stop a pig in a passage--

Give me a stamp and I'll post your eyes back.

marc
He had more spots than a painter's radio.
KIA ORA
POP SWOP

Thanks for extra suggestions of these real-life phrases to Lynn Appleby, Marc Baines, Gordon Wearmouth & Jayne Teasdale. All have ears like Jodrell Bank. —J.B.

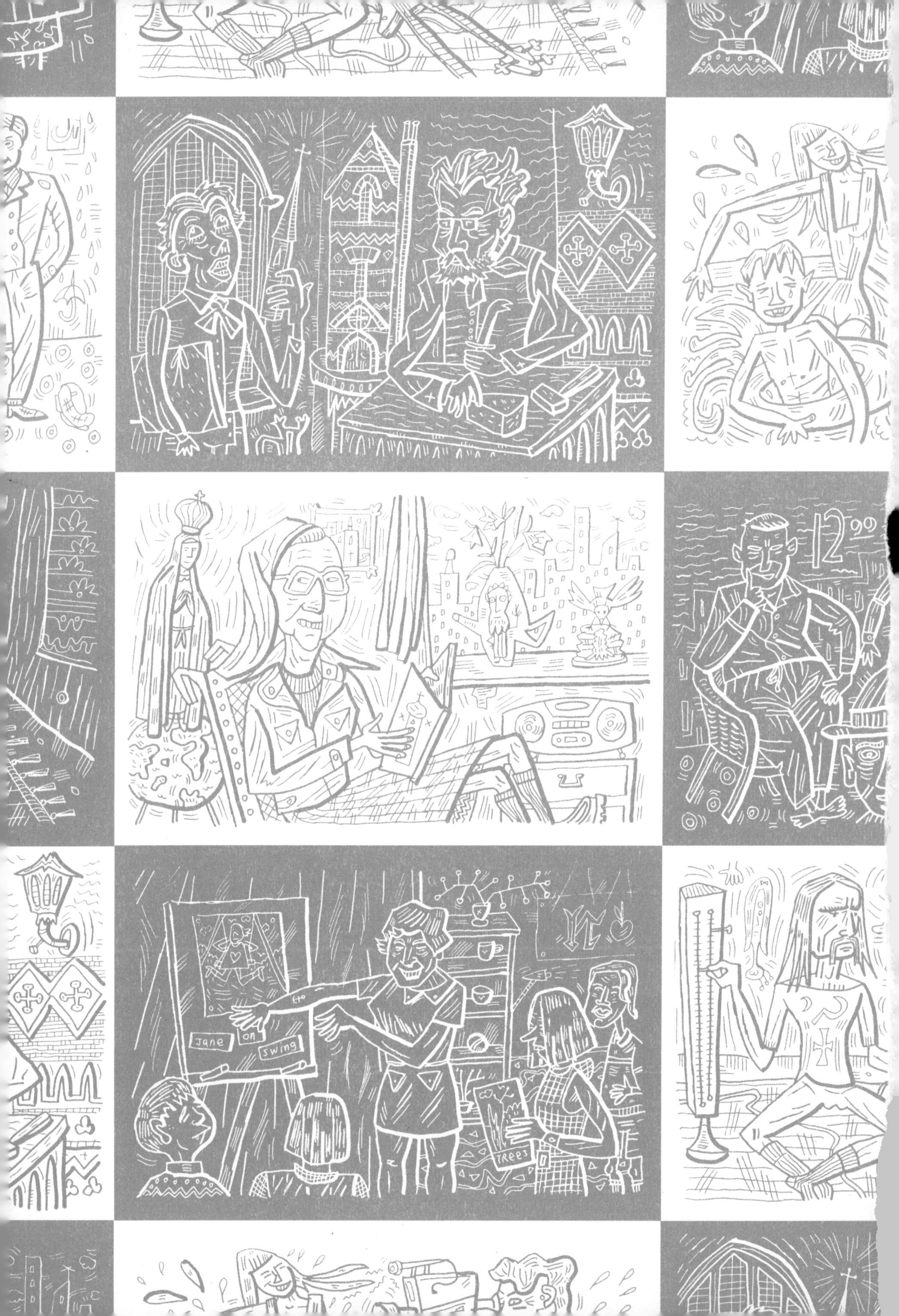
Jane
on
swing
TREES